STORY LAND

A Selection of Favorite Sesame Street Stories

STORY LAND

A Selection of Favorite Sesame Street Stories

A SESAME STREET/GOLDEN PRESS BOOK

Published by Western Publishing Company, Inc.
in conjunction with Children's Television Workshop.

This educational book was created in
cooperation with the Children's Television
Workshop, producers of Sesame Street.
Children do not have to watch the television
show to benefit from this book. Workshop
revenues from this product will be used
to help support CTW educational projects.

Also featuring the Sesame Street cast:
Emilio Delgado as Luis
Will Lee as Mr. Hooper
Loretta Long as Susan
Sonia Manzano as Maria
and Bob McGrath as Bob

Table of Contents

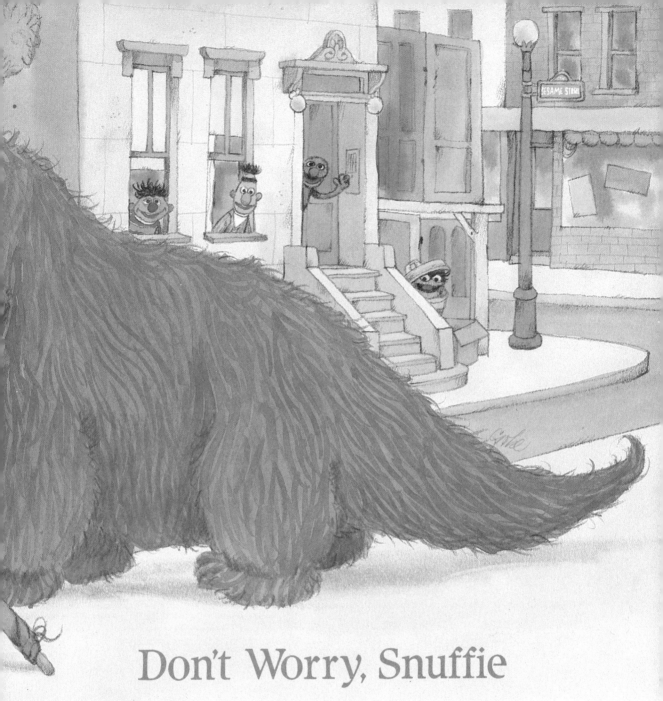

Don't Worry, Snuffie

One hot summer day, a tall yellow bird named Big Bird and a big furry Snuffle-upagus named Snuffie climbed on to the Number 6 Sesame Street bus. Big Bird had a backpack on his back. It was stuffed with two sleeping bags, food, some pots and pans, and a few dishes. Snuffie was carrying a long pole wrapped with canvas. He held it tightly in his snuffle as he made his way to the back of the bus, saying "Excuse me," and "Pardon me." He was being very careful not to bump into anyone.

9

"We are going to have so much fun on our camping trip," Big
Bird said as they found seats on the bus. He unfolded a map
and spread it across his lap. "We are here. The Lazy Days
Campground is here. All we have to do is stay on this bus until
we get there. We can't miss it!"

Snuffie looked at the map. "It looks easy enough," he said.

"Of course it is," Big Bird answered. "Don't worry, Snuffie."

"Where will we sleep, Bird?" Snuffie asked.

"We are going to sleep in our tent," Big Bird said.

"Outside?" Snuffie asked.

"Of course," Big Bird said. "You can't put a tent up *inside*.
Sometimes you are a very silly Snuffle-upagus."

But Snuffie did not feel silly. He felt worried. He had never
been camping before. He had never slept outside before.

It was a long ride to the campground, and Snuffie was worried about missing their stop.

"Bird," he said finally, "we're here!"

Big Bird and Snuffie stepped off the bus and looked around. Big Bird took a deep breath of fresh country air. "Isn't this great?" he asked. "I told you not to worry, Snuffie."

Big Bird led the way as they walked to the campground office. The director said her name was Joan, and she showed them to their campsite.

"If you need any help," she said, "just ask." Then she told them where they could go swimming in the lake.

"There is a lifeguard on duty there," Joan explained. "Just follow the path with the orange signs."

Snuffie and Big Bird waved good-by to Joan.

"Now all we have to do is set up camp," said Big Bird.
"Do you know how to put up the tent?" Snuffie asked.
"Don't worry, Snuffie," said Big Bird. "It's easy. Just watch me."

Snuffie watched. He tried not to laugh when Big Bird got one side of the tent up, and the other side fell down. He tried hard not to laugh when Big Bird got tangled up in the canvas and fell down.

"Why don't I hold the middle pole with my snuffle while you tie the sides down," Snuffie finally suggested.

"Thanks, Snuffie," said Big Bird. "Let's cooperate."

Soon the tent was up and they had unrolled their sleeping bags. Snuffie looked around. The tent was like a little house, he thought. But he wondered what it would be like to sleep in the tent when it was dark outside.

"See?" said Big Bird. "I told you not to worry, Snuffie. It's not hard to put up a tent."

"Now let's go find that place to swim!" said Big Bird.

"Okay," said Snuffie, and he followed Big Bird down the path to the lake.

"Let's just walk across these stones," Big Bird said.

"Gee, Bird," Snuffie said. "They look awfully slippery. Why don't we stay on the path with the orange signs like Joan told us to?"

"Don't worry, Snuffie," Big Bird said. "This is a short cut. Watch me!"

Snuffie watched as Big Bird stepped on the first stone. SPLASH! He fell into the water.

"Quick!" Snuffie cried. "Grab onto my snuffle and I'll pull you out."

In a Snuffle-upagus second, Big Bird was out of the water and on dry land again.

"I think we'd better stay on the path this time," Big Bird said. "Then you won't be worried, Snuffie."

Soon they came to a lovely, sandy clearing beside the lake. They waved to the lifeguard, and the lifeguard waved back.

All afternoon they swam and splashed in the lake. Snuffie used his snuffle to spray water over his back. Then he used his snuffle to squirt Big Bird.

14

"Wasn't it a great idea to go camping?" Big Bird said as they headed back to their campsite.

Snuffie agreed that it was a good idea. In fact, he had so much fun swimming that he had forgotten to worry about sleeping in the tent. But when they reached the campsite, he began to worry again.

"I brought hot dogs and marshmallows to roast over our camp fire," said Big Bird.

"Bird," said Snuffie, "do you know how to build a camp fire?"

"Don't worry, Snuffie," Big Bird said. "It's easy! All I have to do is rub two sticks together. Watch me!"

Snuffie watched as Big Bird found two sticks and began to rub them together. He rubbed and rubbed, but nothing happened.

"Gee," he said. "It always works on television."

Snuffie shuffled off toward the campground office.

"I'll be right back, Bird," he called over his shoulder.

Soon Snuffie returned with Joan. She showed them how to dig a deep pit, and then she started the fire.

"You should always have a grown-up help you build a fire and stay with you as long as the fire is burning," she told Big Bird and Snuffie.

They asked Joan to stay for dinner. She showed them how to roast hot dogs and marshmallows on long sticks over the coals. After dinner they sang songs around the campfire. Joan told Big Bird and Snuffie about the forest paths they could explore the next day.

Then they looked up in the sky and wished on a star. Joan showed them how to find the Big and Little Dipper.

"It's time for me to go back," Joan said. So she showed Big Bird and Snuffie how to put out the fire. They helped her shovel dirt into the pit to make sure the fire was out.

As it got darker and darker, Snuffie got more and more worried. He wished he was back on Sesame Street in his own Snuffle-upagus bed.

"What a great day," Big Bird said as he crawled into his sleeping bag. "I'm exhausted."

Snuffie crawled into his sleeping bag, too. He was surprised by how soft and warm it felt. He snuggled down deep inside it. He lay there very quietly and tried hard not to worry.

Snuffie could hear the gentle rustling of the leaves in the forest. He could hear the sound of a bird in a tree. He began to think about that bird in its nest.

"That bird is camping out, too," he thought. "It is safe and warm in its nest, just like I am safe and warm inside my sleeping bag."

Snuffie began to think about all the other forest animals who were getting ready for bed. He thought about them so hard that he forgot about worrying.

"Good night, Bird," Snuffie said.

"Good night, Snuffie," Big Bird answered.

But a few minutes later, Big Bird was still wide awake.

"Snuffie?" he said.

"Yes, Bird?" Snuffie asked sleepily.

"I can't go to sleep. It's too quiet here. I miss the sounds of the buses and cars and garbage trucks on Sesame Street. I miss my nest. I miss..."

"Isn't your sleeping bag soft and warm?" Snuffie asked.

"Yes," said Big Bird.

"Good. Snuggle down deep inside it," Snuffie said, and Big Bird did. "Now listen," said Snuffie. "Listen carefully. Do you hear the sound of that bird? She's saying, 'Cheep, cheep, go to sleep,' to her baby birds."

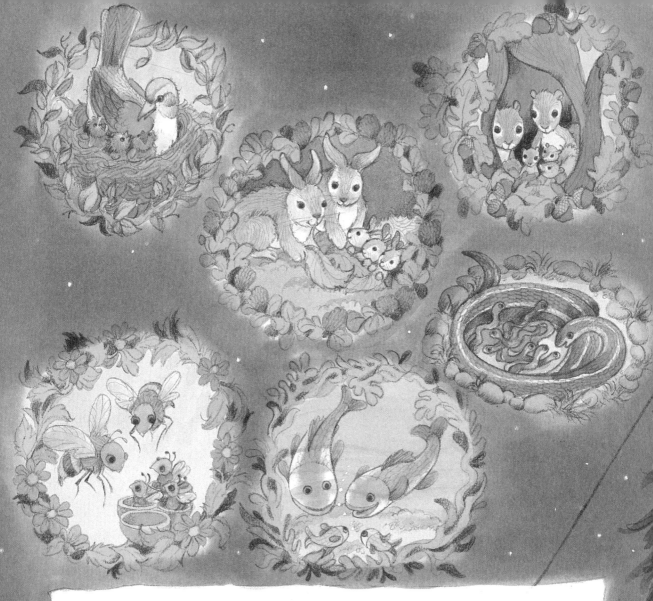

Big Bird listened. He could hear the chirping sound of a bird in the forest.

"Do you know that there are rabbits putting their baby bunnies to bed in rabbit holes all over the forest? There are mommy and daddy squirrels tucking their little squirrels into their beds in their tree homes."

"There are?" asked Big Bird.

"Oh, yes, Bird," Snuffie said. "There are all kinds of wonderful sounds in the forest, and all kinds of very sleepy babies. Bees are telling baby bees to stop their buzzing and shut their eyes. Little snakes are being told to stop hissing and to hush. Even the baby fish stop swimming and splashing as they get ready to go to sleep."

Thinking about all those sleepy babies in their forest homes made Big Bird very sleepy, too.

"Don't worry, Snuffie," Big Bird said dreamily. "I'll be able to go to sleep now."

"Sweet dreams, Bird," said Snuffie.

The Case of the Missing Duckie

The day the duckie disappeared was Ernie's birthday.

Because it was a special day, Ernie had decided to spend it doing things he liked to do. And the thing he liked to do most was take a bath with his Rubber Duckie.

Right after breakfast Ernie went into the bathroom and filled the bathtub with water.

"You know, Rubber Duckie," he said, "you are my very best friend. I could never take a bath without you. Who would I talk to if I felt lonely? Who would cheer me up if I got soapsuds in my eye? Gee, Rubber Duckie, I'm awfully fond of you."

Just then the telephone rang and Ernie went to answer it. "I bet someone is calling to wish me Happy Birthday," he thought.
He left Rubber Duckie on the stool in the bathroom.

"Hello?"

"Hi, Ernie! This is Big Bird. I just called to ask you a question. Are you going to be home at two o'clock this afternoon?"

"Gee, Big Bird, I guess so," said Ernie. "What is happening at two o'clock this afternoon?"

"Oh, nothing," said Big Bird. "I was just wondering if you were going to be home then, that's all. Well, good-by, Ernie."

24

"Hmmm. Big Bird didn't wish me Happy Birthday," thought Ernie. "Maybe he doesn't know that today is my birthday. Gee, maybe no one knows that today is my birthday. Oh, well, I still have Rubber Duckie to keep me company."

When Ernie returned to the bathroom, he had a strange feeling that something was missing.

"Now what could be missing?" he said. "I remembered the soap. I remembered the towel. Rubber Duckie, what did I forget? Rubber Duckie? RUBBER DUCKIE?!"

Ernie stared at the stool where he had left Rubber Duckie.

Rubber Duckie was gone!

Ernie went back to the telephone.

He called his friend Sherlock Hemlock the detective.

"Hello, Mr. Hemlock," said Ernie. "Something terrible has happened. I need a detective."

"I'll be there in a minute," said Sherlock Hemlock.

A minute later there was a knock on the front door and Ernie opened it.

"It is I, Sherlock Hemlock, the world's greatest detective," said the man with the magnifying glass. "What seems to be the trouble?"

"I was going to take a bath when I noticed that something was missing," said Ernie.

Sherlock looked at Ernie very carefully.

"Aha! I have it!" he cried. "Your clothes are missing!"

"My clothes are in the bathroom," Ernie explained.

"Then I will begin looking for your clothes in the bathroom," said Sherlock.

Ernie followed Sherlock Hemlock into the bathroom.

"Gadzooks! I have found the missing clothes," cried Sherlock.

"But my clothes were never missing," said Ernie. "The thing that is missing is . . ."

"The soap!" said Sherlock.

"No, not the soap," said Ernie. "The soap is right here. It is . . ."

"The bathtub!" cried Sherlock.

"No, no, not the bathtub," said Ernie. "It is Rubber Duckie that is missing."

Ernie sighed sadly. "He disappeared while I was in the living room answering the telephone."

"In that case," said Sherlock, "I shall call this case 'The Case of the Missing Duckie'! And I shall begin solving this case by looking for clues in the living room."

30

Ten minutes later Ernie was sitting in the bathtub, staring at the faucet and feeling very sad—because there is nothing sadder than being sad on your birthday—when Sherlock popped in, carrying a big box full of rubber bands.

"The Case of the Missing Rubber Bands is solved!" said Sherlock.

"Gee, Mr. Hemlock," said Ernie. "That's Bert's rubber band collection. His rubber band collection isn't missing."

When Sherlock appeared again his arms were full.

"I, Sherlock Hemlock, have found the missing rubber plant, the missing rubber ball, the missing rubber raft, the missing rubber glove, the missing rubber stamp, and the missing rubber bands."

"I'm sorry, Mr. Hemlock," said Ernie, "but none of those things is missing."

Just then Bert came into the bathroom.

"Hey, Ern," he said, "have you seen my rubber plant, my rubber ball, my rubber raft, my rubber glove, my rubber stamp, and my rubber bands?"

"Everything is here in the bathroom, Bert," said Ernie. "Everything (sniff) except Rubber Duckie."

"Egad!" cried Sherlock. "Don't tell me that Rubber Duckie is missing, too!"

At two o'clock in the afternoon the doorbell rang and Ernie
went to see who was there.

Everybody was there!

"Surprise!" they all shouted.

"We brought you a birthday party," said Big Bird. "That's why
I wanted to know if you would be here at two o'clock."

The kitchen door opened and Cookie Monster came out carrying a big birthday cake.

And right in the middle of the frosting sat... "Rubber Duckie!" cried Ernie. "Am I glad to see you!"

"Me borrow Rubber Duckie for birthday cake," said Cookie Monster.

"Aha!" cried Sherlock. "Cookie Monster borrowed Rubber Duckie for the birthday cake. I, Sherlock Hemlock, have solved yet another cake... I mean, case."

Everyone Makes Mistakes

One day Big Bird was walking along thinking about what he was going to get Mr. Snuffle-upagus for his birthday, when— WHAP!—something cold and wet hit him in the face.

Big Bird had walked right into Susan's fresh clean clothes that she had washed and hung out in the sun to dry—and he knocked the clothesline down. Wet socks and jeans and towels and sheets fell to the ground.

35

"Oh, no! Susan will be so angry with me when she sees her clean laundry all dirty on the ground," said Big Bird. "What will I tell her?"

"Hmm. I could tell Susan that a big flock of birds was flying
south for the winter and flew right into the laundry hanging on
the line and pulled it all down.

"No, that's no good," he said. "Birds fly south in the fall and
it's spring now."

"Let's see," said Big Bird. "I could tell Susan that a giraffe escaped from the zoo and ran straight through the yard and got all tangled up in her laundry and scattered it all over. I could tell her that."

Big Bird thought for a moment. "No. Susan would never believe a silly story about a giraffe escaping from the zoo."

"Maybe I could tell Susan that today was the day of the Great Sesame Street Bicycle Race! I could tell her that the racers rode their bikes straight into her laundry and dragged it on the ground!"

40

"Nah. The Great Bicycle Race was last week. Susan will remember it because she won the race.
"I can't tell her that."

"Well," Big Bird said, "I could say that there was a big fire on Sesame Street. All the fire engines came racing through here on their way to put out the fire and the ladders and hoses got caught on the clothesline and pulled it down."

"No, I can't tell Susan that," he said sadly. "She would know
there wasn't a fire on Sesame Street today."

"How about a circus? That's it! The circus came to perform
right here on Sesame Street and the tightrope walker practiced
her act on Susan's clothesline, and knocked down the clothes."

"Wait a minute. That's a terrible idea. A circus act here in Susan's back yard? I can't tell her that's what happened. I can't blame my mistake on somebody else."

"There could have been a rodeo here today. Rodeo Rosie and her friends were roping steers here. What if I tell her that?"

"No," Big Bird said. "That story is just as silly as the others."

"What happened, Big Bird?" cried Susan, when she saw the mess. "Look at my clean laundry all over the ground!"

"Well...it's like this," stammered Big Bird. "A flock of...no, I mean...a giraffe on a bicycle...no, I mean a circus...or was it Rodeo Rosie in a rodeo...?"

Big Bird stopped. "No, Susan, it was none of those things," he said. "I wasn't looking where I was going and I walked right into your laundry and knocked it down. I'm sorry, Susan. Are you angry?"

"Well," answered Susan, "a little. But I'll get over it."

"I'll help you wash the clothes again," said Big Bird. Big Bird and Susan began to pick up the clothes.

"Don't worry, Big Bird," said Susan, "everyone makes mistakes."

49

How the Twiddlebugs Celebrate the Coming of Spring

The Twiddlebugs live in a flower box under Ernie's window. In the winter Twiddlebug Town is covered with snow. Then there are no flowers, and all of the Twiddlebugs are fast asleep in their cozy little beds.

But in the spring the snow melts and the Twiddlebugs wake up. The very first thing they do, after they brush their twiddles and drink their orange juice, is celebrate the coming of spring!

They begin by having a parade. A parade is a fine idea, because the Twiddlebugs haven't seen each other all winter. Half of the Twiddlebugs march in the parade and half of the Twiddlebugs sit on the sidewalk and watch the parade. In this way, all of the marchers can see all of the sitters and all of the sitters can see all of the marchers. Of course, not all the marchers can see all the marchers and not all the sitters can see all the sitters, but this isn't a problem because everyone can see everyone at the picnic.

The picnic is also a fine idea, because the Twiddlebugs haven't had anything to eat all winter.

After the picnic is over, the most important part of the celebration begins. Some of the Twiddlebugs who are especially good at twiddling start to play a lovely tune. The rest of the Twiddlebugs make a big circle. They begin to dance. Their dance is called The Flower Dance.

The Flower Dance goes something like this: all of the dancers hold hands and circle around—faster and faster. When the music ends, all of the dancers fall down.

The Twiddlebugs believe that their Flower Dance will bring the flowers back to Twiddlebug Town.

A long time ago there were no flowers in Ernie's window box. One day the Twiddlebugs were dancing in a circle and a wonderful thing happened. Right after they all fell down a shower of seeds fell out of the sky and landed in the soil around Twiddlebug Town. Soon the window box was full of beautiful flowers.

Spring was followed by summer, and summer was followed by fall, and the Twiddlebugs all crawled into their little cozy beds and went to sleep.

When they woke up months later, the flowers were gone.
Nobody knew what had happened.
Nobody knew what to do.
Then the wisest of all the Twiddlebugs stepped forward and said: "Do you remember last year when we were dancing and the flower seeds fell out of the sky? If we want flowers again, we must dance again."

So the Twiddlebugs began to dance. They all held hands and circled around—faster and faster. When the music ended, they all fell down.

It was at that very moment that Ernie decided it was time once again to plant some flower seeds in his window box. He took a big handful of seeds and sprinkled them into the box.

The Twiddlebugs did not see Ernie. They only saw the seeds fall out of the sky.

And that is why every year, when the Twiddlebugs celebrate the coming of spring, they do the Flower Dance.

Marshall Grover Meets the (Gulp) Noon Train

As Marshall Grover rode into Sesame Gulch one morning, he heard the Count calling to him from the telegraph office.

"Good morning, Count," said Marshall Grover. "Have you read any good telegrams lately?"

"Yes, I have," said the Count. "As a matter of fact, I have read five good telegrams already this morning. And, only a moment ago, I read one fascinating telegram addressed to *you*. Listen to this: 'Meet the noon train — or else!' The telegram is signed 'M'!"

Marshall Grover took off his white hat and mopped his brow with his bandana. "Or else?" he said. "What does that mean?"

"I don't know," said the Count.

"Signed M?" asked Marshall Grover. "Count, does the telegram explain who M is?"

"How could it explain?" cried the Count. "The telegram has only six words. Look. I will count them for you. 'Meet' is one word, 'the' is two words, 'noon' is three words. Ha, ha, wonderful, wonderful. 'Train' is..."

"Thank you, Count. It is very nice of you to count the words for me," said Marshall Grover. "But right now I have another problem. I do not know anyone named M."

"Well, there are many people whose names start with M," said the Count. "M could be Mean Mary, the rustler. That is one person. M could be Mad Montana Max, the bank robber. Ha, ha, that is two people whose names start with M. Wonderful, wonderful. M could be the Mysterious Masked Bandit..."

"Please, Count," said Grover. "All those M's sound very (gulp!) scary. I do not want to go alone to meet a very scary M." Grover pulled out his pocket watch. "It is now eleven o'clock. The noon train will be here in one hour. Will you go with me to meet (gulp!) M?"

"No, I cannot," cried the Count, "and there is one very good reason why I cannot. The good reason is ... counting. That's it! I have to stay here and count the words as they come over the wires." He spun around and vanished into the telegraph office. The door slammed shut behind him.

"Well, that is a good reason," said Grover. "I will find someone else to go with me."

From a distance came sounds of hammering, and muffled cries of "Ouch!"

"Big Bird!" said Marshall Grover. "Of course. Big Bird will go with me." He hurried down the street and into Luis's Harness Repair Shop.

Big Bird looked up from the saddle he was trying to fix. "Oh, hi, there, Marshall Grover. Did I hear you calling my name?"

"Yes, Big Bird," said Grover. "I have received a very exciting telegram. Listen to this: 'Meet the noon train — or else! Signed M'."

Big Bird gasped and dropped the tack hammer on his foot. "Ouch!" he cried. "That smarts!"

"Oh, my goodness!" said Grover. "Now, as I was saying, I have received this very exciting telegram, and I thought it would be fun if a bunch of us got together and went down to the depot to meet..."

Big Bird was shaking his head very hard. "Oh, I don't think so, Marshall Grover. I mean, I have so much to do right here. I really don't have time. Busy, busy, busy," he muttered.

Marshall Grover looked at his pocket watch. "Well, it is only eleven-fifteen," he said. "I still have forty-five minutes to find someone who will go with me to meet the noon train."

57

Marshall Grover set off down the street toward the Livery Stable. "I will ask Oscar to meet M with me. Maybe that is something a Grouch would like to do."

Oscar was in his rain barrel by the stable door. "I heard that," he shouted. "Oh no, not me. I'm not going to meet any stupid train."

"But, Oscar," said Marshall Grover. "I thought you were my friend."

"Listen, Grover," said Oscar. "Friendship is a two-way street. So you stay on your side of the street, and I'll stay on my side. Okay?" The lid of Oscar's rain barrel slammed shut.

Marshall Grover looked at his pocket watch again. "Oh," he gasped, "it is eleven-thirty. Only thirty minutes until noon. I must hurry and find someone who will go with me to meet (gulp!) M."

59

60

Right across the street, Ernie and Bert and a bunch of cowpokes were lounging in front of Hooper's General Store.

"Ernie and Bert!" exclaimed Marshall Grover, hurrying over to Hooper's. "My good friends Ernie and Bert. Surely they will not let me down."

"Ernie and Bert!" he cried. "Guess what! I have wonderful news. M is coming and we must all hurry down to the depot to meet the noon train."

"Right!" said Ernie. "I do have to hurry—but not to the depot. I have to hurry home. I just remembered that I promised Rubber Duckie I'd give him a bath this morning. So long!" He lit out in the direction of the 123 Ranch.

"Gee, that reminds me," said Bert. "I have to hurry and feed my pigeons." He rushed off in the other direction.

"And we have to hurry and poke some cows," mumbled all the others. They ran to the hitching post, jumped on their horses, and galloped madly in all directions.

"Hey! Are they scared?" gulped Grover. He looked at his watch. "Fifteen minutes before twelve!" He mopped his forehead with his bandana and looked around wildly. "Will nobody go with Grover to meet the noon train?"

61

Suddenly, there came the sound of galloping hooves, a cloud of dust, and a hearty, "Whoa, there, Silver!" Prairie Dawn, Pony Express Rider, galloped up Main Street and slid to a halt in front of Hooper's General Store.

"Howdy, Marshall Grover," she hollered, leaping off Silver and shouldering the U.S. Mailbags. "How's everything?" But before Grover could answer, Prairie Dawn had disappeared into the store with the mail.

"Prairie Dawn is very brave," said Marshall Grover to himself. "She would not be afraid to go with me to meet (gulp!) M."

In a moment, Prairie Dawn came racing out of Hooper's General Store with the new sacks of mail. She threw them over Silver's back and leapt into the saddle.

"Wait, Prairie Dawn!" called Grover. "Please stay and go with me to meet the noon train."

"I heard all about that telegram ya got," said Prairie Dawn, reining in Silver with one hand. "There's nuthin' I'd like better than to go with ya to the depot and give that lowdown sidewinder M a piece of my mind. But I'm carryin' the U.S. Mail, and the U.S. Mail must go through. Neither snow, nor rain, nor M on the train shall stay this Pony Express Rider from her appointed rounds. Giddyap, Silver!" she cried. They whirled around and were gone.

Marshall Grover looked up and down the street.

No one was in sight. Dust hung thick in the air from the sudden departures of his friends.

There was no sound of a friendly voice, no hammering from Luis's Harness Repair Shop, no clinking of soda glasses in the General Store. Only a shutter somewhere flapping in the wind, and the rustle of the tumbleweeds rolling down the empty street.

Then ... far off ... but coming nearer, he heard the mournful whistle of a train, the (gulp!) noon train.

Marshall Grover looked at his watch. "Five minutes before noon!" he cried. "Oh, no. I must go to the depot all by myself."

He pulled his hat brim down low over his eyes, tucked his thumbs into his belt, and marched bravely down to the depot.

Grover stood alone on the creaky platform, his heart pounding beneath his badge, his feet shaking in his boots.

The train came chuffing slowly down the line and stopped with a screech and a sigh. Great clouds of steam rose from around the wheels. Grover looked at his watch. It was exactly twelve noon.

Marshall Grover pulled off his bandana and mopped his brow as he waited for the passengers to get off. He waited, and he waited. "Hey, maybe M missed the train!" he said.

Suddenly a big carpet bag bounced down the passenger car steps and landed, THUD, on the platform at Grover's feet. A pair of silver-toed boots stepped down from the train. "Oh, there you are," said a voice. Grover gulped and slowly looked up. There, right next to him, stood...

"Mommy!" cried Marshall Grover. "Mommy, Mommy, Mommy! M is for Mommy! Mommy is a person whose name starts with M! Oh, Mommy, I am so glad to see you!"

"Hello, there, Grover," said his mommy. "I see you got my telegram."

"Oh, yes, Mommy, I did," said Grover. "But why did it say, 'Meet the noon train—*or else*'?"

"Because," said his mommy, "I wanted you to meet me *or else* I would not have known where to get off the train."

"I see, Bert," said Ernie. "But Bert, why are you going to sell oatmeal to people?"

"It's all part of my plan, Ernie, part of my plan. Just listen to this..."

Bert looked to the left and the right. "Come closer, Ernie," he said. "I don't want anyone else to hear this. Are you ready?" And he began to whisper in Ernie's ear.

"First I'm going to set up my stand. See, it has a little stove and everything. I bought this big sack of oatmeal this morning with the money from my piggy bank." He pointed to a big sack of oatmeal on the table.

Don't Count Your Pigeons

Ernie came down the steps of 123 Sesame Street and there, right in front of the building, Bert was busily tacking a sign onto a table. "Hey, Bert, old buddy," he said, "what are you doing?"

"Oh, hi, Ernie," said Bert. "I'm setting up an oatmeal stand. Isn't it great?"

"Sure, Bert, it's great. What's an oatmeal stand?"

"Come on, Ernie," said Bert. "An oatmeal stand. You know—a place where you sell steaming hot bowls of delicious oatmeal to people."

"I'm going to cook the oatmeal right here at my stand, Ernie. People will smell it cooking, and it will smell so delicious that they'll just have to buy some. And so many people will buy my oatmeal that I'll make a lot of money—all the money that I'll need!"

"Well, that's nice, Bert," said Ernie, "but why do you need a lot of money?"

"To pay the captain, Ernie! To pay the captain of the boat."
Bert's voice was getting louder.

"What boat, Bert?" said Ernie.

"The banana boat, Ernie, the banana boat. The one that's
going to bring my 25 crates of bananas!"

"Well, that's nice, Bert," said Ernie, "but what are you going to
do with 25 crates of bananas?"

"I'm not going to do anything with the bananas, Ernie," said Bert, smiling proudly. "I'm going to use the *crates* to build 25 pigeon coops. Isn't that terrific?"

"And by the time I finish my coops," Bert continued, "my pigeon eggs will be ready at the Pigeon Exchange."

"What pigeon eggs, Bert?" asked Ernie.

"The ones I ordered, Ernie. The ones I ordered from the J.C. Pigeon Company. I'll go down to the Pigeon Exchange and pick them up. That's 12 dozen pigeon eggs. Think of it, Ernie—144 pigeon eggs!"

"I am thinking of it, Bert," said Ernie. "I am thinking of it."

73

74

"Why, I'll have the biggest and best pigeon farm in the whole neighborhood," Bert went on. "Maybe I'll even keep the oatmeal stand going so I can make more money to buy more banana crates and pigeon eggs. Of course, you'll have to handle that part, Ernie. I'll be too busy raising and training pigeons to take care of the business side of things any more."

"Gee, Bert," said Ernie, "I don't think I want…"

But nothing could stop Bert now.

"I'll be famous, Ernie. I'll get my picture in *The Pigeon Fanciers' News*. I'll be invited to lecture on pigeon raising at Rhonda's Rest. I'll even go on a lecture tour, Ernie. Maybe I'll even go around the world telling people about my pigeon-raising methods. Think of it, Ernie. The WHOLE WORLD!"

And as Bert said "the WHOLE WORLD," he threw his arms out wide in excitement and ... SMACK! He knocked his sack of oatmeal off the table. Oatmeal spilled everywhere—all over the sidewalk and into the street.

"Help, Ernie," cried Bert. "My oatmeal! My pigeons! My pigeon farm! Oh, no!"

Suddenly Bert gasped. Pigeons began swooping down from everywhere. And before they knew it, Ernie and Bert were surrounded by a whole flock of pigeons happily pecking away at the oatmeal on the ground.

"How about that, Bert!" said Ernie. "You haven't had one oatmeal customer yet, and you already have your pigeon farm—right here on Sesame Street!"

FRESH HOT
OATMEAL
25¢ a bowl

The Monster
in the Mirror

One day a shaggy, big, blue monster was walking down Sesame Street. He was carrying a big bag of cookies. "Yum," he said, "me can hardly wait to gobble up all these delicious cookies!"

Suddenly he stopped. "Hey," he said, "that very interesting. Me not know there a door here. Hey, and who that shaggy, big, blue monster in there?"

"Hey, monster," said the first shaggy blue monster, "me Cookie Monster. What *your* name?"

But the other monster did not answer.

"Hey, monster," said Cookie Monster, "where you get such a big bag of cookies? It look as big as mine."

Again the other monster did not answer.

"Hey, monster," said Cookie Monster, "why you not answer me? That really very rude. Me getting a little angry."

Still the other monster did not answer.

"Hmmm," thought Cookie Monster, "that monster not too smart. Me play a trick on that monster and get his cookies."

"Hey, monster," said Cookie Monster, "me really want to be friends. Put down your bag of cookies and let's shake paws. Look, me put down cookies."

Cookie Monster started to put down his bag of cookies, and so did the other monster.

"Good," thought Cookie Monster. "Me pretend me going to shake paws, and grab big bag of cookies instead."

Cookie Monster lunged toward the other bag of cookies. SMACK! He bumped right into something hard. CRUNCH! He sat down, right on his own bag of cookies.

Cookie Monster slowly got up and picked up his flattened bag of cookies.

"Oh, no!" he said, looking inside the bag. "Now cookies all crumbs."

And do you know what? The very same thing happened to the other monster.

"Hey, monster," said Cookie Monster, "you know how to make crumb cake?"

But the other monster did not answer.

"Well," said Cookie Monster. "Me just have to make crumb cake all alone. Hmmm…me wonder if chocolate chip crumbs make good crumb cake.…"

The Day
Herry Monster
Held Up the Stage

Sesame Gulch was a sleepy little Western town. Not much ever happened there. Except—there *was* the day that the rumor got started. The rumor was that Herry Monster was going to hold up the stage!

Fearless Ernie and the Alphabet Kid rushed to tell Sheriff Bert the news.

"Guess what, Bert!" said Ernie as he came in the door.

"I'm not interested in guessing games today, Ernie," Bert said. "This is an important day. Today my pet pigeons are arriving on the stage. It's due any minute."

"That's just it, Bert. The stage is going to be a little late."

"LATE? Why is the stage going to be late, Ernie?" shouted Bert.

"Because," answered Fearless Ernie, "Herry Monster is going to hold up the stage."

Ernie stood on the steps of the Sheriff's Office
and looked down the main street of Sesame Gulch.
He saw a number of leading citizens of the tiny
town, going about their business.

"Hey, everybody!" he called.

They all stopped to listen.

"Herry Monster is going to hold up the stage. So
let's get up a posse and get over to Hootenholler
Pass!"

Marshall Grover, who had just ridden into town,
strode over from Franklin's Livery Stable.

"That is absolutely right, Fearless Ernie," he said.
"Do not fear! I, Marshall Grover, and my Wonder
Horse, Fred, will accompany you!"

"Me, too," said Big Bird, who was standing
nearby in the street, practicing fancy rope tricks
with his lasso.

In a matter of minutes the brave citizens of Sesame Gulch had formed a posse to head off Herry at the pass. They galloped off in a cloud of dust.

On one side of the narrow trail through
Hootenholler Pass, the Jinx Gang and Herry Monster
were hiding behind rocks and bushes, lying in wait
for the stagecoach.

On the other side of the trail, the posse hid behind
more rocks and bushes and lay in wait for the
desperadoes.

The sun was high when they all heard the
rumbling of horses' hooves and stagecoach wheels on
the rocky trail. But they heard a louder rumbling,
too—the sound of 500 stampeding cattle!

"Hey, Bert," said Ernie from behind a mesquite
bush, "here comes a stampede!"

"Oh, no!" Bert groaned, peeking out from behind a
big boulder. "Oh, no! Not today! Not the XYZ
Ranch's annual cattle drive north! Those cattle are
going to stampede right in the path of the stage!
Somebody do something!"

The stagecoach and the charging herd of cattle raced toward Hootenholler Pass.

Herry Monster jumped out from his hiding place and hoisted the stagecoach over his head as the XYZ cattle thundered underneath.

"Look, Bert," said Ernie. "Herry Monster *held up the stage!*"

"Look, Ernie!" replied Bert. "My pigeons are flying away!"

"They're not flying away, Bert," said Ernie. "They're flying home. They're homing pigeons, Bert."

As Herry set the stagecoach down gently on the trail, a cheer went up from the Sesame Gulch posse. But the Jinx Gang was not cheering.

"When I said to hold up the stage, *that's* not what I meant!" the leader of the gang shouted at Herry. Then the desperadoes jumped on their horses and galloped toward Texas.

And no one in Sesame Gulch ever forgot the day that Herry Monster held up the stage.

93

Ernie and Bert's Summer Vacation

One hot, steamy afternoon at 123 Sesame Street, Ernie sat looking through his collection of travel folders. He was trying to figure out where he and Bert should go for their summer vacation. Suddenly, Bert rushed in. He had just come from Bennie's Bargain Basement and a sale on rubber thong beach sandals.

"Guess what, Ernie!" shouted Bert. "I bought *three* thongs for the price of *one!* Some terrific bargain, huh, Ernie?"

"I guess so, Bert," said Ernie, "if you happen to have *three* feet. Tee hee hee. Say, Bert, have you ever been to Walla Walla, Washington?"

Only then did Bert notice that he was surrounded by a monumental mess. There were travel folders everywhere!

"Ernie! Explain this mess!"

"Mess? What mess, Bert? We have to decide where we're going on our vacation, don't we? Well, I've got a few places in mind, Bert."

"I can see that, Ernie," Bert muttered as he waded through the sea of folders and sank into his favorite armchair.

And where did Ernie and Bert finally decide to go?

Why, the very same place they went to last year and the year before that—the seashore!

"You and Rubber Duckie can ride the waves in your rubber raft, Ernie," suggested Bert.

"Right, old buddy. And you can comb the beach for rare bottlecaps!" said Ernie. "So let's get packing!"

Suddenly, Ernie began racing around the apartment, madly emptying closets and drawers. Bert couldn't believe his eyes. Ernie was packing everything in sight—his miner's helmet, his ski poles, the moosehead, his hockey stick...

"Ernie," said Bert, "you don't need all this stuff!"

"You never know, Bert. You just never know," Ernie replied.

"Come on, Ernie!" cried Bert. "You can't possibly use a hot water bottle at the beach!"

"You never know when it might come in handy, Bert."

"Ernie, you're packing everything but the kitchen sink!"

"Sorry, Bert, but there's no room for the sink. Not if we're taking the living room rug."

Ernie and Bert piled all their things into their car and they were off! Bert was at the wheel. Ernie sat beside him, strumming his ukulele.

"This is the life, old buddy," said Ernie. "I can feel that warm, silky sand between my toes already."

"Um, I hope it doesn't rain like last year," Bert said cautiously.

"Not a chance!" said Ernie.

Ernie and Bert drove for a long time.

"Which way to the beach, Bert?" asked Ernie.

But Bert had dozed off with the map spread out on his lap.

Then Ernie spotted a sign which read, "Don't miss it!!
Mt. Baldy."

"Hmmm," he thought. "I've always wanted to see Mount
Baldy! We'll just take a *little* side trip." He turned and followed a
winding road higher and higher into the mountains.

"Where are we?" asked Bert, waking with a start.

"At the Mount Baldy Lookout, just in time for the sunset," said Ernie. "Let's look through these viewers, Bert, so we can see Mount Baldy close up. Are you looking at Mount Baldy, Bert?"

"Uh huh," said Bert. "But I can't see it. There are too many clouds."

"Gee, Bert, I can see it very clearly. It's tall and kind of egg-shaped. And right on the tippy top there's a big hairy bush. *Hairy?* Wait a minute! Something's strange here."

Ernie looked around the side of his viewer and exclaimed, "Guess what, Bert! I've been looking at the back of your *head!*"

The sun had sunk behind the mountains. By the time they reached the highway it would be dark. So Ernie suggested they spend the night in the woods.

"Absolutely not, Ernie!" said Bert, alarmed at the prospect. "Besides, we didn't bring any camping equipment."

"Sure we did, Bert." Then Ernie began to load Bert down with all their baggage.

"Hey, Ernie," cried Bert, staggering under his heavy burden. "How come *you're* not carrying anything?"

"One of us has to blaze the trail, Bert. Follow me!" said Ernie, as he charged into the woods.

They found a pleasant campsite by a stream, and Ernie set to work immediately.

"Hand me the carpet, Bert." Bert did so gladly. "Now the ski poles, please. Stand by with that hockey stick, Bert."

In no time at all, Ernie had made a tent out of the living room rug, using the ski poles and hockey stick to hold it up.

"Try out the tent, Bert," said Ernie. "I'm going fishing for our dinner."

Ernie soon returned with some Baldy Mountain Speckled Trout. After a delicious dinner, Ernie and Bert crawled into the tent for the night.

"Well, here we are, snug as two bugs in a rug!" said Ernie. "Good night, Bert."

"Sleep tight, Ernie."

On their way down from the mountains the next morning, they stopped at a monument of a pioneer family.

"Gee, they sure were funny looking back in those days, huh, Bert?" said Ernie.

"I don't know what you mean, Ernie. They look fine to me—handsome, in fact."

PIONEER FAMILY MONUMENT

Bert had been driving for some time when Ernie noticed a strange change in the scenery.

"Uh, Bert, I think we've taken a wrong turn somewhere."

"Don't bother me when I'm driving, Ernie."

"But, Bert, this looks like *Africa*!"

"When I'm at the wheel, I don't play silly games, Ernie. I keep my eyes on the road."

"Look Bert," cried Ernie. "There's a hippo."
"Sure, sure," said Bert, still staring straight ahead at the road.
"Look, a giraffe!" Ernie cried.
"Oh yeah, and I suppose there's an orangutan, too."
"Right, Bert. How did you know?"

Even Ernie didn't know that a lion had jumped into the back of the car and was having a wonderful time looking through Bert's binoculars. Suddenly, the lion spotted the big moosehead beside him. With a frightened roar, he leaped out of the car. "What was that?" shrieked Bert, finally looking around.

"Ernie," he cried, "we're in a jungle! Help!"

"That's what I've been trying to tell you, Bert."

Bert stepped on the gas, and they zoomed out of there as fast as they could.

YOU ARE NOW LEAVING Jennifer's Drive-In Jungle... COME AGAIN !!

It had been an exhausting morning, so they decided to stop for a snack at a diner called Colonel Mustard's Last Stand.

Bert had a bowl of lukewarm oatmeal and Ernie had pancakes.

Later, they stood under the statue of Colonel Mustard. "Isn't he a handsome fellow?" Bert remarked.

"Look," said Ernie, pointing up to a sign in the Colonel's hand. "The sign says it's only five miles to the beach. Let's get going!"

Finally, they arrived at the beach! Bert put on his rubber thongs, and he and Ernie climbed over a high dune. There, at last, was the sparkling ocean.

"Looks just like the picture in the travel folder, huh, Bert? This is a peach of a beach!"

HOT DOGS

Bert looked around for signs of rain. There were none, so he carefully spread his beach towel on the sand. "Ah, peace and quiet—nothing to do but watch the waves," he sighed contentedly.

"Say, Bert. Want me to make you a sand castle?" Ernie asked.
"I want to take a long nap, Ernie," yawned Bert.
"Fine. You do that, old buddy. And by the time you wake up, the sand castle will be all done."

When Bert woke up, he found that he was buried in a huge pile of sand with only his head sticking out.

"Ernie! What's going on here?" he bellowed.

Ernie was busy digging a moat around Bert.

"See, I made you a sand castle, Bert! Now I think I'll go and get some hot dogs and soda pop. See you later, Bert."

"Ernie, get me out of here!" yelled Bert. "I don't want to be a sand castle. I want some lunch! Ernie, come back! My nose itches! Ernie . . . I think it's going to *rain!*"

Finally, Ernie returned with the hot dogs and soda.

"I see you've made a feathered friend, Bert," Ernie observed. "Sorry to be so long, but there was a big line at the hot dog stand."

"It's starting to rain, Ernie," moaned Bert.

"Don't worry, Bert," said Ernie. "I'll take care of everything." He pitched a beach umbrella over Bert's head and sat under it with him.

"Gee," said Ernie, handing Bert a Figgie Fizz, "isn't this fun? Aren't you glad we decided to come to the beach?"

Look Before You Lift

One day Grover was strolling past the park looking up at the trees and the beautiful blue summer sky when he tripped and fell over something.

"Oh, my goodness," he said, getting up and brushing off his fur. "What is this big laundry bag doing right in the middle of the sidewalk? Somebody must have dropped it on the way to the laundromat. I, friendly, helpful pal Grover, will take this laundry to the laundromat where it belongs. Oh, I am sure that the person who lost this laundry will be very happy to see it again."

"Oh, my goodness!" exclaimed Grover as he tried to pick up the laundry bag. "What a big bag. I cannot even lift it."

He grabbed the rope. "Aaaargh!" he said, as he tried to pull the bag along the sidewalk. "I cannot budge this bag. This laundry is certainly very heavy.

"Yikes!" he said, as he tried to kick the bundle along the sidewalk with his foot. "And this laundry is very hard, too."

"It is time for a rest," said Grover, sitting down on the bag. "It is nice to be helpful," he said, "but in this case it is also very difficult. This bag is so big and heavy and hard that I cannot lift it or pull it or kick it along with my foot. How can I take it to the laundromat if I cannot move it?"

Just then, Roosevelt Franklin came along.

"Oh, Roosevelt Franklin," said Grover, "I am so glad to see you. Would you help me get this heavy, heavy bag of laundry to the laundromat?"

"I'll try," said Roosevelt.

So they each took one end of the bag and tried to lift it , but it was too heavy.

"Grover," said Roosevelt Franklin, "are you sure this bag has laundry in it? Let's take a look inside to make sure."

"Of course it has laundry in it," said Grover. "It is a laundry bag. We do not need to waste time looking in it. We need to hurry and take it to the laundromat where it belongs. Come on, try again, Roosevelt!"

First Grover pulled and Roosevelt Franklin pushed. Then Roosevelt Franklin pulled and Grover pushed. Then they both pulled and then they both pushed. But they still couldn't budge that heavy bag.

"Oh, my goodness," gasped Grover. "We need more help!"

So they sat down on the bag and waited.

Pretty soon Betty Lou and Cookie Monster came along. Then Grover and Roosevelt Franklin pulled and Cookie Monster and Betty Lou pushed. But nothing happened.

"Hey," said Betty Lou, "what's in this bag?"

"Maybe it lots of very heavy cookies?" said Cookie Monster.

"Do not be silly," said Grover. "Does this look like a cookie bag? Of course not. It looks like a *laundry bag!* Now here we go. Everybody grab one corner and we will pick up this bag and take it to the laundromat together!"

Each one took a corner and tugged and tugged, and they managed to lift the bag just clear of the sidewalk.

"Hurry," gasped Grover. "I cannot hold on for long."

They staggered down the sidewalk toward the laundromat.

"Oh," gasped Betty Lou, as they stumbled down the curb and crossed the street.

"Help," cried Roosevelt Franklin as they almost ran into a tree.

"Look out!" shouted Cookie Monster as a boy on a skateboard nearly knocked them over.

"Aaaah," they all sighed, as they dropped the bag in front of the laundromat.

Just then, Herry Monster came running down the street toward them. "Hey, anybody see a great big bag?" he shouted angrily. "Somebody took my bag while I was napping."

"Oh, hello, Herry," said Grover. "Ahem. Is this your laundry bag? I found it near the park and we have brought it to the laundromat for you."

"That's my *bag*," said Herry, "but it doesn't have *laundry* in it."

"It doesn't?" said Grover.

"If you'd have bothered to look inside you wouldn't have found laundry, Grover. You would have found my *weight-lifting equipment!*" said Herry, throwing the bag over his shoulder. "I go to the park to exercise with my barbells and dumbbells every day. Ya."

The Count
Counts a Party

One day the Count sat in his castle amidst all the things he liked to count, and he was very sad.

"Woe is me," he said. "I cannot think of anything new to count. I have counted everything! I have counted:
    Dogs and cats,
    Frogs and bats,
    Plants and rocks,
    Pants and socks.

Fleas and mice,
Peas and rice,
Chairs and clouds,
Hairs and crowds.
I've counted big,
I've counted small.
There's nothing left to count at all!"

He sobbed.
"One sob," said the Count.
And he sighed.
"One sigh," said the Count, "and one teardrop! Alas, what is there left for me to count?"

He thought of everything he could possibly count, beginning with the letter A and going through the alphabet.

"Aardvarks I have counted, ants I have counted," he said. "Apples I have counted...." He went on until he reached the letter P. "Parades I have counted, parasols I have counted, parrots I have counted, parties... *I have not counted!*"

"That's it! *Parties!*" shouted the Count, startling his pet bats. "I have never counted parties. Eureka! I will give a party for all my friends on Sesame Street...and I will *count the party!*"

"Yay!" said the bats, fluttering about his head in happy circles. "Party, party, party! We're going to have a party!"

And the Count began to prepare for his party.

First he cleaned the castle from basement to belfry. He borrowed a broom from the witch next door and swept all the dust into a big pile, and then swept the big pile under a big rug.

"One sweep, two sweeps, three sweeps, four sweeps!" said the Count. "Ah-ah-ah!"

Then he took down all the dirty old cobwebs and hung up clean new cobwebs.

He even told his bats to take a bat-bath in their bat-tub.

"Lyuba," he said to his number-one bat, "don't forget to wash behind your wings. You, too, darlings."

"Don't worry," said the bats, "we'll get squeaky clean. Squeak, squeak, squeak!"

133

"Now," said the Count, "I will have nineteen friends from Sesame Street at my party. That makes twenty friends, counting me. (And I *love* to count me!) So I will need twenty plates. Ah-ah-ah! And twenty party balloons! Ah-ah-ah! And a party hat for everyone! Twenty party hats! Ah-ah-ah-ah!

"And what else?" asked the Count. "I know! Something to eat!"

First, he baked a chocolate layer cake, and then he counted the twenty lovely layers.

134

"Nobody should eat just cake," said the Count, "so we'll have some fruit! Twenty apples. Twenty! And twenty peaches. Twenty! And for the big eaters...twenty watermelons!"

Then he set the table with twenty plates, and it was time for the party to begin!

The Count let down the drawbridge. On the front path to his castle he laid out twenty welcome mats. Then he waited for his friends.

He waited...and waited...and waited...and waited. Nobody came!

"Woe is me!" said the Count. "I have waited twenty minutes and nobody has come to my party. What have I done wrong?"

"Woe is us, too!" said his bats. "No party, no party, no party!"

"Wait!" said the Count. "I know why nobody has come. I forgot to invite them!"

136

And, like a flash of his own lightning, he sat down and wrote twenty invitations (one for himself, too) saying, "Stop everything and come right away—1,2,3—to my castle for a party. Come as you are. Do not even change your clothes. Hurry, hurry, hurry! Signed, Your Friendly Local Count."

He gave the invitations to his bats, who flew off to deliver the invitations to Sesame Street.

When Ernie and Bert got their invitations, Ernie was in the bathtub and Bert was waiting to take his bath. They started right out to the Count's castle.

Cookie Monster was eating a box of delicious cookies when he got his invitation. He ate the invitation, too, and then dashed off to the party.

Big Bird was playing hopscotch, so he hopped all the way to the party.

Super-Grover was flying around looking for someone in distress when Lyuba delivered the invitation. He sped to the castle with his cape streaming behind him, and landed in the moat.

141

Twenty minutes after he sent the invitations, the Count looked out the castle door and saw the whole gang coming up the path.

"Aha!" said the Count. "My friends are coming. I knew I could count on them!"

"Yay!" said the bats, as they flew back into the castle. "It's party time!"

142

"Wait! Not so fast, my pets," said the Count. "I must count everybody!"

So, while everyone waited patiently, the Count counted his guests.

"1,2,3,4,5,6,7,8,9,10,11,12,13,14,15,16,17,18,19...only 19? But there should be twenty. Who is missing? Oh, of course. I forgot to count myself! How silly of me! I, the Count, make twenty. Twenty playful party people! Ah-ah-ah-ah!"

"And twenty batty bats!" shrieked the bats. "Strike up the band!"

As the band played the Transylvania Polka twenty times, everybody danced and ate and danced some more and ate some more. The party lasted for twenty hours, and the Count was very, very happy.

"One! One *wonderful* party!" exclaimed the Count ecstatically. "Ah-ah-ah-ah-ah-ah!!!"

Vegetable Soup

"Oh-me-oh-my, me so hungry!" said Cookie Monster. He had been to the supermarket and was waiting for his groceries to be delivered.

"All me think about is cookies—beautiful Big Newtons! Oh! Where groceries? Where COOKIES??"

Then the doorbell rang.

"Me *eat!*" cried Cookie Monster, running to the door.
A delivery girl handed him a box of groceries.
Cookie Monster looked into the box. "Hey! These not Big
Newtons. These not even cookies. What we have here?"

Cookie Monster tried to figure out what the things in the grocery box were.

"Long skinny orange thing look like pencil," he said, looking at a carrot. "Me sharpen it and write word 'cookie.'"

So he sharpened the carrot in a pencil sharpener and tried to write "cookie," but it didn't make a mark.

"Hmm. Maybe not pencil. Maybe telescope!"
So he put the carrot to his eye, but he couldn't see a thing.
"Wait! Me know!" he said, picking up the whole bunch of
carrots. "Long orange things all go together, and they are...hat!"
And he put them on his head.

Then Cookie Monster took out the celery and tried to use it as a back scratcher, but it didn't work.

"Hmmm," he said, "this must be a bunch of pretty flowers!"

And he put it in a vase.

Next he tried to use the broccoli as a feather duster, but that didn't work, either. So he put it in the vase with the celery.

He picked up a beet and started it spinning like a top.

"Round and round and round it go," said Cookie Monster. "Where it stop, nobody know!"

Then he found a squash and put it to his ear.

"This must be telephone. Hello, operator?" he said, speaking clearly into the squash. But there was no reply.

Cookie Monster held up an onion. "Small, white, round thing must be ball for playing jacks." So he tried to play jacks with the onion, but it wouldn't bounce.

Then he took out some potatoes. "Hmm, these funny looking things! Cowabunga!" he yelled and began to juggle the potatoes.

And just as he got them all in the air, Ernie and Bert came in
with some bags of groceries.

"Me smell cookies!" yelled Cookie Monster, forgetting to juggle
the potatoes. "Where you get cookies?"

"The supermarket made a mistake and sent your cookies to us
and our groceries to you," said Bert.

"These things groceries?" cried Cookie Monster. "Hat, flowers, top, telephone, balls for jacks, things for juggling?"

"They're *vegetables*," said Ernie, as he and Bert began to gather them all up.

"This isn't a hat," said Bert, taking the carrots off Cookie Monster's head. "These are carrots."

"Hey, Ernie, why you take flowers out of vase?" asked Cookie Monster.

"These aren't flowers," said Ernie. "This is celery, and that is broccoli."

"And this is a beet, not a top," said Bert, as he stopped the spinning beet.

"You need to call somebody?" Cookie Monster asked when Ernie picked up the squash. "Don't bother. That telephone out of order."

"This isn't a telephone," said Ernie with a sigh. "It's a squash."

"Well, squash out of order."

Then Bert found the onion. "Hey, that my jacks ball!" Cookie Monster exclaimed.

"Don't be silly," said Bert. "It's an onion."

"And you were juggling potatoes!" said Ernie. "You do funny things with vegetables."

"What me supposed to do with them?" asked Cookie Monster.

"Make vegetable soup, of course," said Bert.

"Oh ... what that?"

"Gosh, Cookie Monster," said Ernie. "You've never heard of vegetable soup? It's delicious!"

"Vegetable soup as delicious as cookies?" asked Cookie Monster.

"More delicious than cookies," said Bert. "And almost as good as instant oatmeal."

"More delicious than cookies!" cried Cookie Monster. "Quick! Show me how to make vegetable soup! Please!"

So Ernie and Bert took the vegetables into the kitchen. First Bert washed all the vegetables.

"Is it soup yet?" Cookie Monster asked.

"Oh no, Cookie Monster," replied Bert. "We have to cook all the vegetables first."

So Bert put a pot of water on to boil. Then he cut up the carrots and potatoes and Ernie dropped them into the pot.

Then Bert chopped up the celery and Ernie dropped it into the pot.

"Is it soup yet?" asked Cookie Monster.

"Not yet," said Bert, as he cut up the broccoli.

Ernie dropped the broccoli into the pot.

Then Bert sliced the beet and the squash and Ernie dropped them into the pot.

"Mmm, vegetable soup smell good," said Cookie Monster.

"This is really hard work," said Ernie as Bert peeled and cut up the onion. "Hurry up, Bert. I'm hungry."

Then Ernie put the onion in the pot, and Bert added salt and pepper.

Finally, when the soup smelled just right, Bert turned off the stove.

"Is it soup yet?" asked Cookie Monster.

"Yes," said Bert. "The vegetable soup is cooked."

"Now we eat?" asked Cookie Monster.

"Not yet," said Ernie, putting the pot of soup on the table. "It's too hot to eat. You have to let it cool."

162

"But me so hungry!" moaned Cookie Monster. "Me can't wait much longer!"

He stared at the steaming pot of soup.

"Me know!" said Cookie Monster, snapping his fingers. "Me help cool soup."

So he started blowing on the soup.

Pretty soon Cookie Monster was out of breath, so he started fanning the soup with a newspaper.

"There must be easier way to cool soup," he said. "Aha! There is!"

And just as he aimed an electric fan at the soup, Bert shouted, "Wait, Cookie Monster! Don't do that. It's cool enough to eat now."

164

"SOOOUP!" yelled Cookie Monster, and he picked up the pot, opened his mouth, and swallowed all the vegetable soup in one big gulp.

"Mmm. Curiously refreshing," he said, wiping his mouth. "So that what to do with vegetables. Very interesting. Now me show you what to do with cookies.

"COOOOKIE!"

And he picked up the grocery bags and swallowed all the cookies.

"Cookies delicious!" sighed Cookie Monster. "And you right, Ernie and Bert. Vegetable soup delicious. Now, what for lunch?"

A Day in the Life
of Oscar the Grouch

My name is Oscar the Grouch and this is the street where I live. I bet you think that being a grouch on Sesame Street is a lot of fun. Well, let me tell you something. A day on Sesame Street is just like any day on any other street.

BUMP! BUMP! BUMP! At six o'clock every morning the newspaper carrier delivers newspapers to the building next to my can. What a terrible noise to wake up to. I love it. It's that BUMP! BUMP! BUMP! that gets me off to a nice grouchy start every morning.

At seven o'clock in the morning I eat breakfast. Today I'm having orange rinds, rotten eggs, burned bacon, and stale bread crumbs. What a great meal! But I'm sure the breakfast at your house is just as good.

Eight o'clock in the morning is one of those nice times in the day when a grouch can really relax. Everyone is hurrying to school or to work. Rush, rush, rush! No one can stop to say hello.

Isn't it wonderful?

The mail carrier comes at nine o'clock. Today she delivers four letters to the Count. Once again, there is no mail for me. So who wants a silly old letter, anyhow?

Ten o'clock in the morning is clean-up time on Sesame Street.

I can't stand clean-up time. I keep thinking, "There goes another great collection of trash."

At eleven o'clock in the morning some of the people around here do chores and errands.

Bert does his laundry at the laundromat.

Biff takes his paycheck to the bank.

It's twelve o'clock noon, and that's lunch time. I don't know about your neighborhood, but on Sesame Street friends share their lunches. But grouches don't share. I would hate to part with any of my delicious peanut butter and sardine sandwich.

At one o'clock, right after lunch, it's nap time. Even Barkley takes a nap. I just happen to like to play my trombone at one o'clock in the afternoon. Can I help it if Barkley doesn't appreciate great trombone playing?

At two o'clock in the afternoon a lot of people go to the park. There's just one thing I don't understand. The joggers and walkers and bird watchers and kite flyers like to visit the park on a nice sunny day.

I only go to the park when it rains.

By three o'clock in the afternoon most of the kids are home from school and playing games. They're all doing things they like to do.

Around this time I do something I like to do, too. I complain. We grouches don't like to see anyone having a good time.

174

At four o'clock on Tuesday the bookmobile comes to Sesame Street. Well, it is now four o'clock on Tuesday and that is why I am standing in a line in this crowded bookmobile. I am waiting to check out my favorite book—*Mother Grouch Rhymes.*

At last! My favorite time of day! Rush hour!

At five o'clock in the afternoon everyone who has been somewhere else working all day begins rushing home. Cars are stuck in traffic. People are tired and hungry. Motors are rumbling. Tummies are grumbling. Even cheerful people are a little bit grouchy.

Isn't it wonderful?

At six o'clock in the evening I eat my supper. I suppose you eat your supper in the evening, too.

Tonight I am having pizza. Now I ask you, is there anything more delicious than pizza with banana slices on top?

At seven o'clock in the evening Ernie takes his bath.

Here at Oscar's can it's also bathtime, but not for me. Slimey, my pet worm, takes his bath at seven o'clock, too.
Of course, he takes a mud bath. Heh heh heh.

At eight o'clock it's storytime. Over at Big Bird's nest Big Bird reads to all the little birds. They just love a good book. Personally, I can't stand happy endings.

Whew! Now it's bedtime—nine o'clock. Everybody turns out the lights. Everybody snuggles into bed. At last—peace and quiet.

Now it is time for me to practice my trombone again.

What a perfect ending to another yucchy day on Sesame Street.

The Big Game

"Oh, Big Bird," sighed Betty Lou one day as she and Big Bird were sitting together on the steps of 123 Sesame Street. "It's so boring just sitting here. What can we do to have some fun?"

"Let's play a game, Betty Lou," said Big Bird. "Let's play hide-and-seek. It's my favorite game. You be 'it' and count to ten, and I'll hide. I bet you can't find me."

"Okay, Big Bird," said Betty Lou, covering her eyes. "Go ahead and hide. One, two, three..."

The first time, Big Bird hid behind Oscar's trash can, but Betty Lou found him right away.

The next time, Big Bird hid behind the lamppost, but Betty Lou found him right away.

Then Big Bird hid behind the mailbox, but Betty Lou found him right away.

"Big Bird," said Betty Lou, "I don't think hide-and-seek is the game for you. You're just too big to hide all of you in one place. Something always sticks out."

Right across the street some kids were jumping rope. "I think I would like that game," said Big Bird. "It looks like fun."

So Big Bird asked the kids to let him take a turn.

When they swung the rope the first time, it got caught on his beak.

When they swung the rope the next time, it got caught on his tail feathers.

Then the rope got all tangled up in his big feet.

"Big Bird," said Betty Lou, "I don't think jump rope is the right game for you, either. You're just too big for the rope to twirl around you."

186

They started to play hopscotch, but Big Bird's feet were too big for the squares.

They tried to play leapfrog, but Big Bird was so big that nobody could leap over him.

"Oh, Betty Lou," said Big Bird. "I can't play any of these games. I'm going back to my nest."

Just then Prairie Dawn came looking for the Sesame Street gang. She wanted them to go to the park to play games.

Everybody wanted to go except Big Bird. "I'm not very good at games," he said. "I'm too big."

"Come on, Big Bird," said Betty Lou. "Give it a try. I'm sure there'll be a game that is fun for you."

And Betty Lou was right. There were lots of games going on in the park, and one of them was perfect for Big Bird—*basketball.*

All the players wanted Big Bird to be on *their* basketball team.

"Who, me?" said Big Bird. "I've never played basketball before."

"Don't worry," said Roosevelt Franklin, "it's easy. All you have to do is bounce the ball as you run to the basket, and then throw the ball through the hoop."

"Like this?" asked Big Bird, running toward the basket. And he was so tall that he tossed the ball right into the basket without even having to jump.

And all during the game Big Bird scored a basket every time he got the ball!

189

"Big Bird," said Betty Lou when the basketball game was over, "you were the star of the big game!"

"Gee," said Big Bird, "I guess sometimes it's better to be bigger."

190